moOOo!

To Natalie and Ella.
—D. P.

To my mother, who sang with gusto every morning
before breakfast, and who never ceases to believe.
—H. D. K.

Library of Congress Cataloging-in-Publication Data is available.
Library of Congress Control Number: 2013948781

ISBN 978-1-939775-01-6

13 12 11 10   1 2 3 4 5 6 7 8 9 10

Printed in the United States of America

Little Pickle Press, Inc.
3701 Sacramento Street #494
San Francisco, CA 94118

Please visit us at www.littlepicklepress.com.

The Cow in Patrick O'Shanahan's Kitchen

By Diana Prichard

Illustrated by
Heather Devlin Knopf

Little Pickle Press

Patrick O'Shanahan dragged his feet to the kitchen for another boring breakfast.

He didn't see it at first,
but it was definitely there.

A **COW** was in the kitchen!

Patrick stared at the cow. The cow stared back.

Patrick's father strode into the kitchen. Patrick expected him to scream and shout, but he . . . did nothing.

"How about World Famous French Toast for breakfast, Paddy?"

Patrick's jaw dropped. "I . . . guess so."

"We'll need three eggs."

Patrick rummaged in the refrigerator. He looked beside the apples and pushed aside the ranch dressing.

He peered behind the orange juice and . . .

BAGAAAAAWK

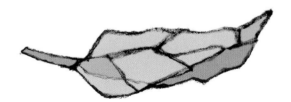

With eyes as big as dinner plates,
Patrick peered back into the refrigerator.

An egg sat on the shelf right where
the chicken had been, and behind it perched
two more fluffy, feathery chickens.

Patrick's hand trembled as he passed
the warm brown egg to his father.

Tap, TAP, crack. "One," his father sang.

Patrick reached for the second chicken, and then
the third. He gently lifted their feathers.

"BAGAAAAAAAWWWWKKKKK!"

Tap, TAP, crack. "Two," his father sang. "And three!"
The last egg plopped into the bowl.

"Now," his father added, "milk."

The cow stepped in front of the refrigerator.

"Excuse me," whispered Patrick.

Drip, driiip, SPLAT! The cow slobbered on the floor.

"Excuuuuuse ME!" Patrick said a little louder.

The cow chewed its cud.

Patrick climbed under the cow.

He had a hunch, so he grabbed the measuring
cup and gently squeezed one of the long
pink teats dangling from the udder. Warm,
frothy milk squirted into the cup.

Patrick proudly handed the milk
to his father, who added it to the eggs,
and began to whisk.

Careful not to step on the chickens or
bump into the cow, Patrick toted a stack
of plates, pair of glasses, and handful
of silverware to the table.

"Don't forget the syrup," his father called.
"We can't have French toast without syrup."

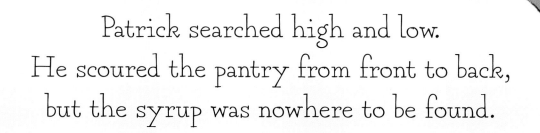

Patrick searched high and low.
He scoured the pantry from front to back,
but the syrup was nowhere to be found.

When he looked back into the kitchen, tall trees with
long bare branches filled the room from wall to wall.
Something sticky trickled down their trunks.

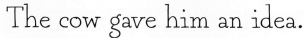

The cow slurped its tongue up and down
one of the trees. Patrick watched closely.

The cow gave him an idea.

Patrick licked the tree and grinned from ear to ear.
"It's syrup! IT'S SYRU P!" he shouted at the cow.

A tiny spigot halfway up the trunk
dripped syrup. Patrick shoved a jar under
the stream and filled it to the top.

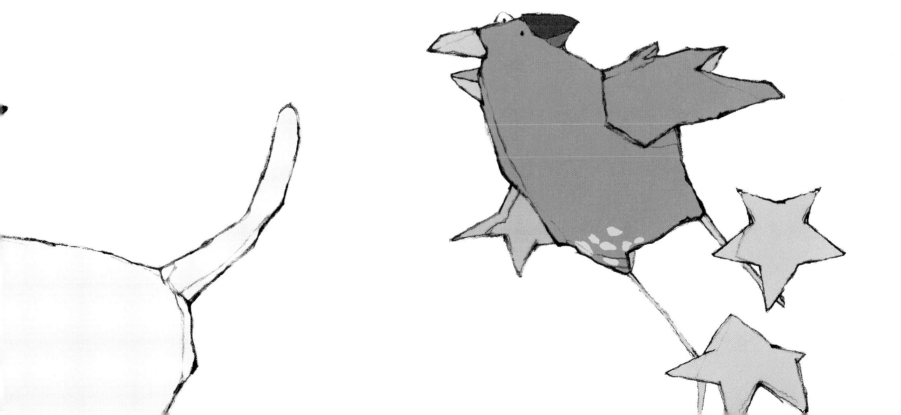

He took it to the table, where his father
was waiting with the tallest stack of
World Famous French Toast he'd ever seen.

Patrick poured the syrup over his French toast . . .
and the trees began to shrink.

He took a bite. A chicken disappeared.

By the time Patrick had eaten through his stack
of French toast, even the cow was gone.

The next morning when Patrick woke up he could barely contain his excitement. He jumped out from under the covers. Wild ideas of where today's food would come from danced through his head.

But as Patrick raced to the kitchen
for another amazing breakfast,
something stopped him in his tracks.

Did he smell . . . bacon?

Author's Note

When kids come to our farm they're usually amazed, excited, and disgusted all at once. It's not uncommon for every emotion from happiness to horror to show up during one farm tour, and I can always count on kids to tell me exactly how farming looks from the outside. It may sound a bit overwhelming, but it's why talking to kids and their families about food and farming is one of my favorite parts of being a farmer. Over the years, we've had lots of kids visit our farm and while none of them were Patrick, many of them inspired this story of him and his crazy breakfast adventures.

This is why I hope you'll join me at www.patrickoshanahan.com to continue this conversation. There you'll find up-to-date resources, fresh family-friendly recipes, and even a kids' section to keep little eaters engaged.

Wishing you happy food and farm adventures,
Diana

About the Author

Diana Prichard is a food and agriculture writer and a farmer who brings bacon into the world, raising pigs from farrow to finish on her small Michigan farm. She lives and works with her husband, Ben, and their two daughters, Natalie and Ella. To learn more, visit www.dianaprichard.com.

About the Illustrator

Heather Devlin Knopf believes that, like a smile, art is universal, with the potential to push imaginations and grow minds. Her earliest art-work, kept tucked away by a thoughtful aunt, dates back to the age of two—a tall red house with nine crooked windows. Today her two young boys, Liam and Lucas, inspire her daily as boundless creators. To learn more, visit www.heatherknopf.com.

Our Mission

Little Pickle Press is dedicated to helping parents and educators cultivate conscious, responsible little people by stimulating explorations of the meaningful topics of their generation through a variety of media, technologies, and techniques.

Little Pickle Press
Environmental Benefits Statement

This book is printed on Appleton Utopia U2:XG Extra Green Paper. It is made with 30% PCRF (Post-Consumer Recovered Fiber) and Green Power. It is FSC®-certified, acid-free, and ECF (Elemental Chlorine-Free). All of the electricity required to manufacture the paper used to print this book is matched with RECS (Renewable Energy Credits) from Green-e® certified energy sources, primarily wind.

Little Pickle Press saved the following resources by using U2:XG paper:

trees	energy	greenhouse gases	wastewater	solid waste
Post-consumer recovered fiber displaces wood fiber with savings translated as trees.	PCRF content displaces energy used to process equivalent virgin fiber.	Measured in CO_2 equivalents, PCRF content and Green Power reduce greenhouse gas emissions.	PCRF content eliminates wastewater needed to process equivalent virgin fiber.	PCRF content eliminates solid waste generated by producing an equivalent amount of virgin fiber through the pulp and paper manufacturing process.
20 trees	9 mil BTUs	1,725 lbs	9,355 gal	626 lbs

Calculations based on research by Environmental Defense Fund and other members of the Paper Task Force and applies to print quanities of 8,000 books.

B Corporations are a new type of company that use the power of business to solve social and environmental problems. Little Pickle Press is proud to be a Certified B Corporation.

Other Award-Winning Books from Little Pickle Press

The Owner's Manual for Driving Your Adolescent Brain
Written by JoAnn Deak, Ph.D. and Terrence Deak, Ph.D.   Illustrated by Freya Harrison

Spaghetti is NOT a Finger Food (and Other Life Lessons)
Written by Jodi Carmichael   Illustrated by Sarah Ackerley

BIG
Written by Coleen Paratore   Illustrated by Clare Fennell

Ripple's Effect
Written by Shawn Achor and Amy Blankson   Illustrated by Cecilia Rebora

Snutt the Ift: A Small but Significant Chapter in the Life of the Universe
Written and Illustrated by Helen Ward

Your Fantastic Elastic Brain: Stretch It, Shape It
Written by JoAnn Deak, Ph.D.   Illustrated by Sarah Ackerley

Sofia's Dream
Written by Land Wilson   Illustrated by Sue Cornelison

What Does It Mean To Be Safe?
Written by Rana DiOrio   Illustrated by Sandra Salsbury

What Does It Mean To Be Present?
Written by Rana DiOrio   Illustrated by Eliza Wheeler

What Does It Mean To Be Green?
Written by Rana DiOrio   Illustrated by Chris Blair

What Does It Mean To Be Global?
Written by Rana DiOrio   Illustrated by Chris Hill

www.littlepicklepress.com